An Egg for Meg

CATHERINE MALASKI

Meg had a hen.

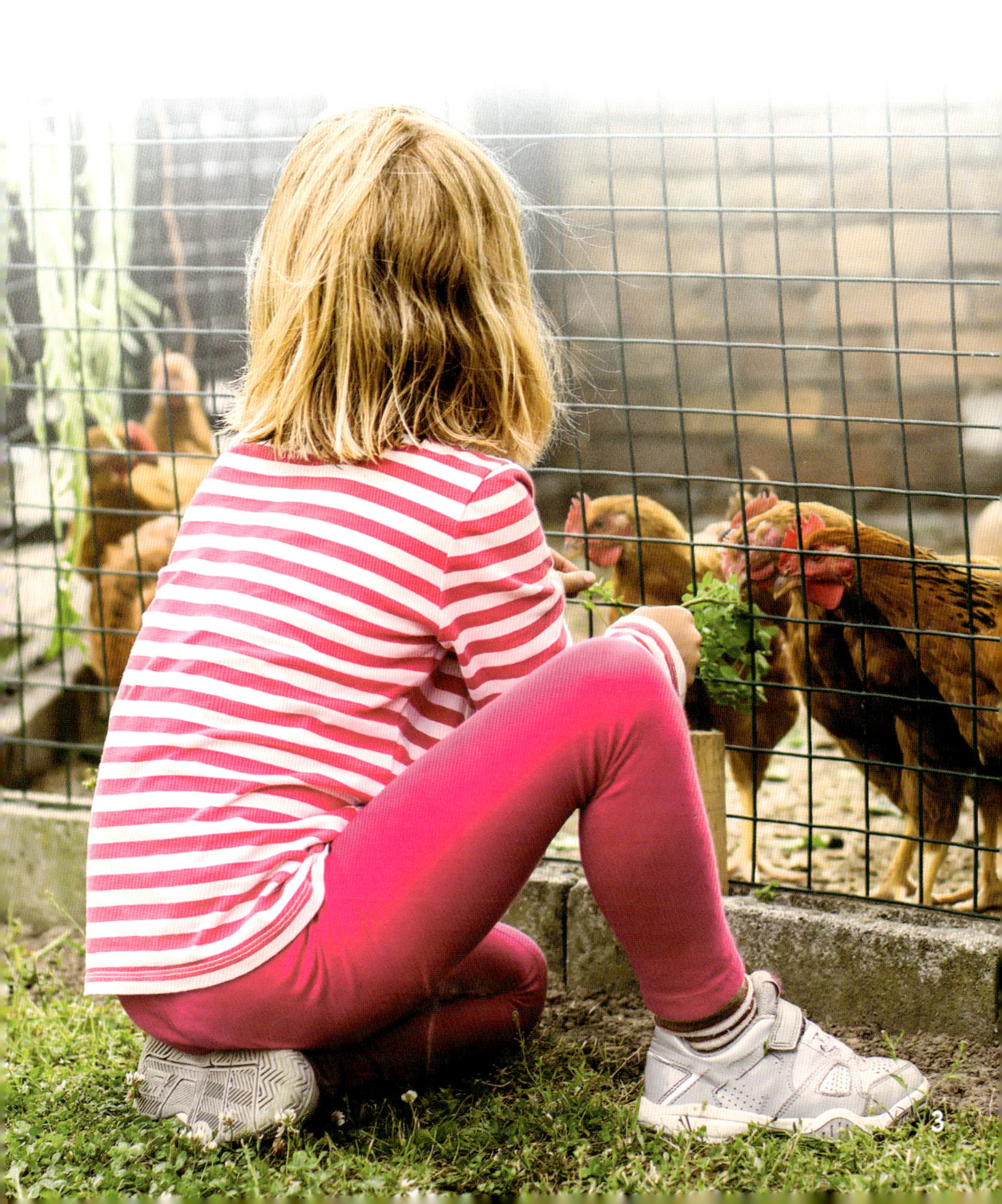

The hen had
ten eggs for Meg.

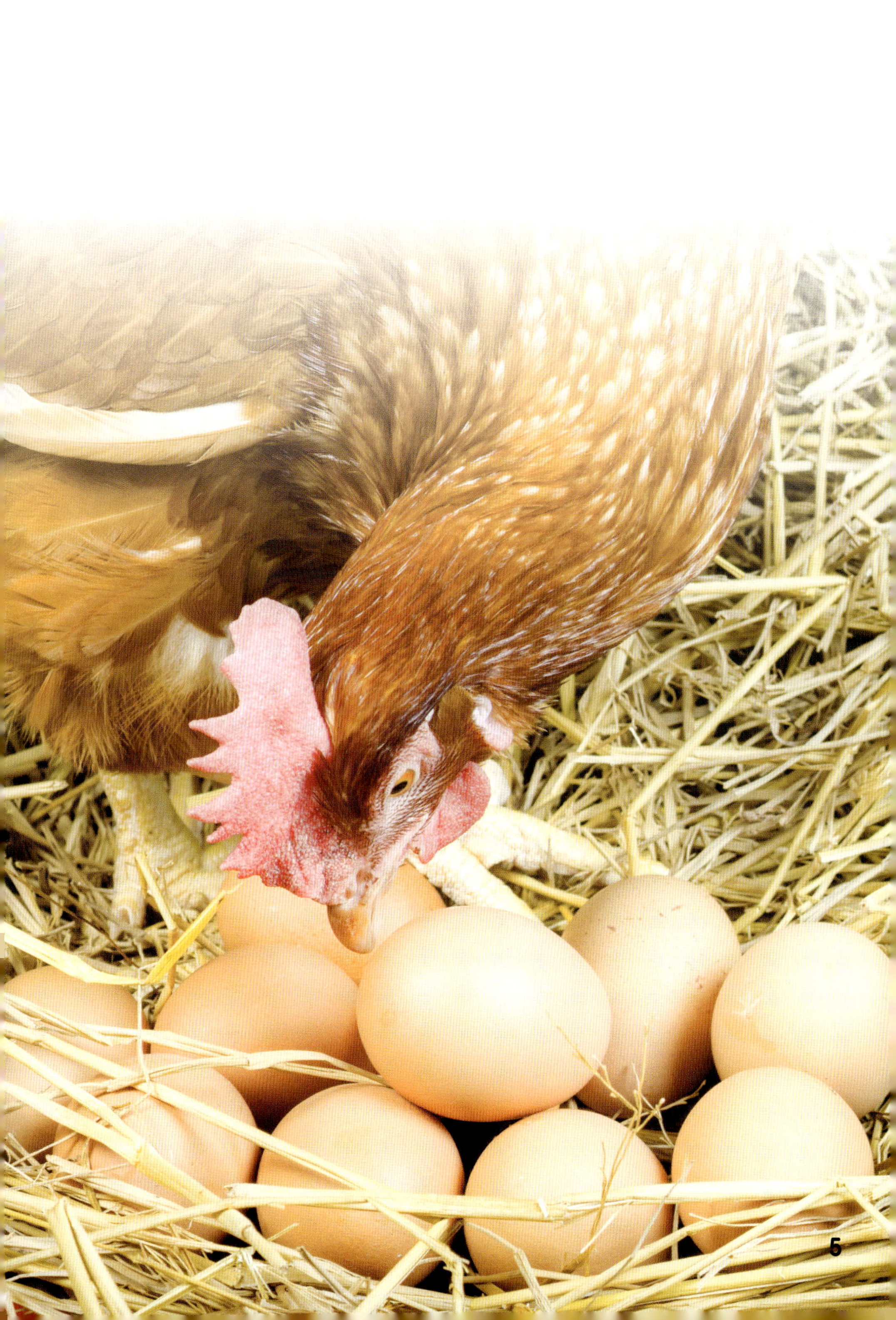

Meg got an egg.

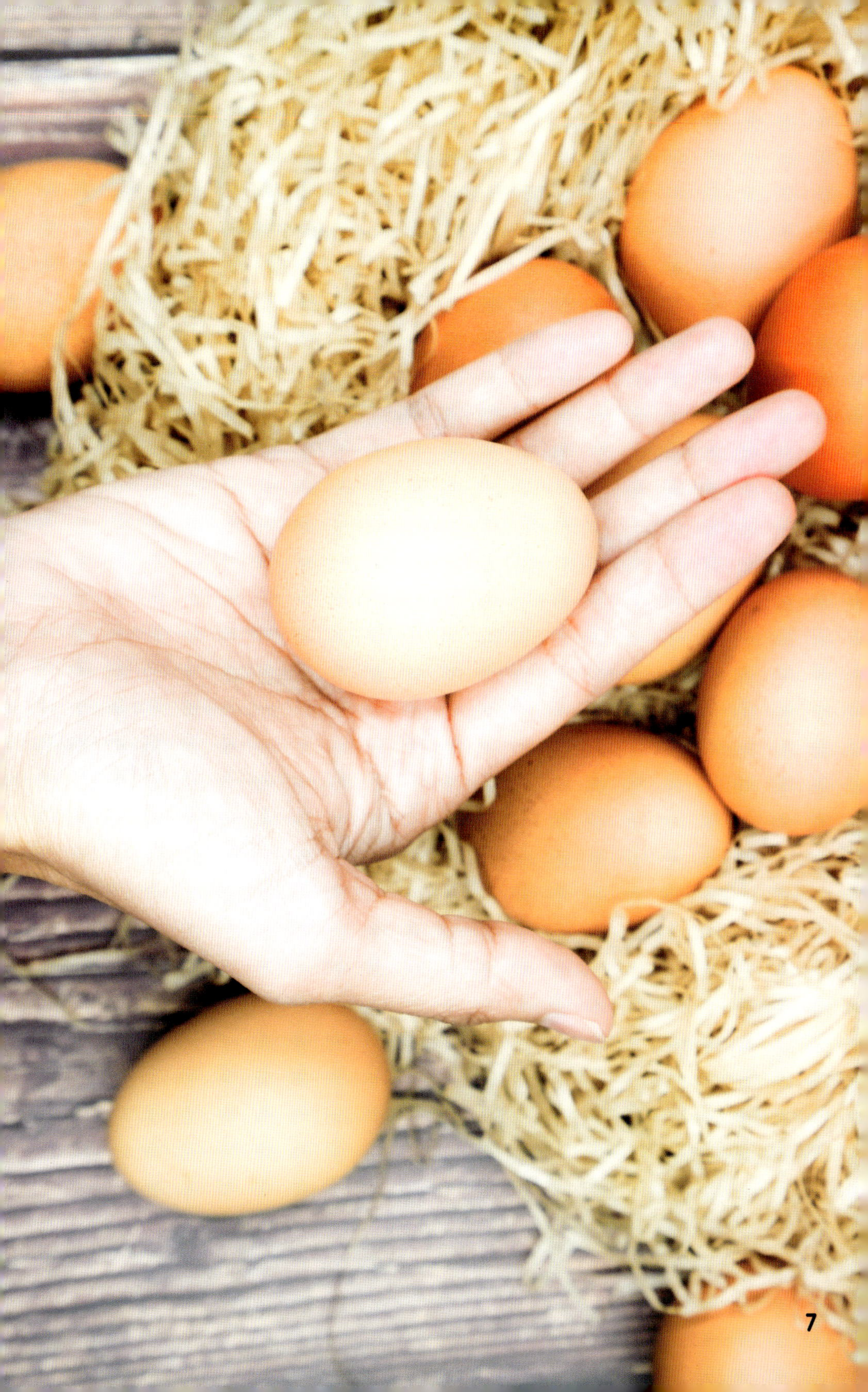

Meg set the egg in
a cup.

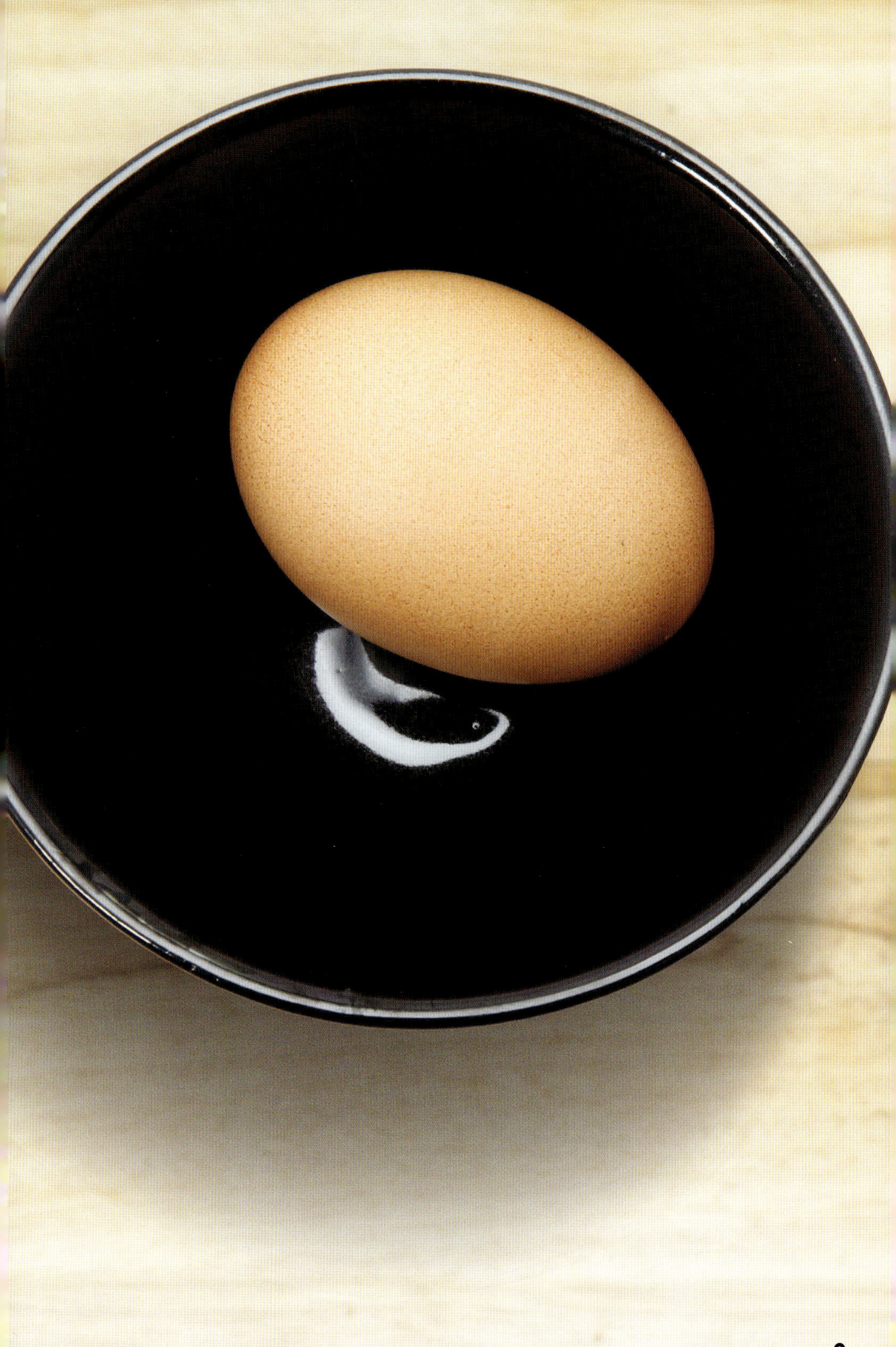

Meg let the pot
get hot.

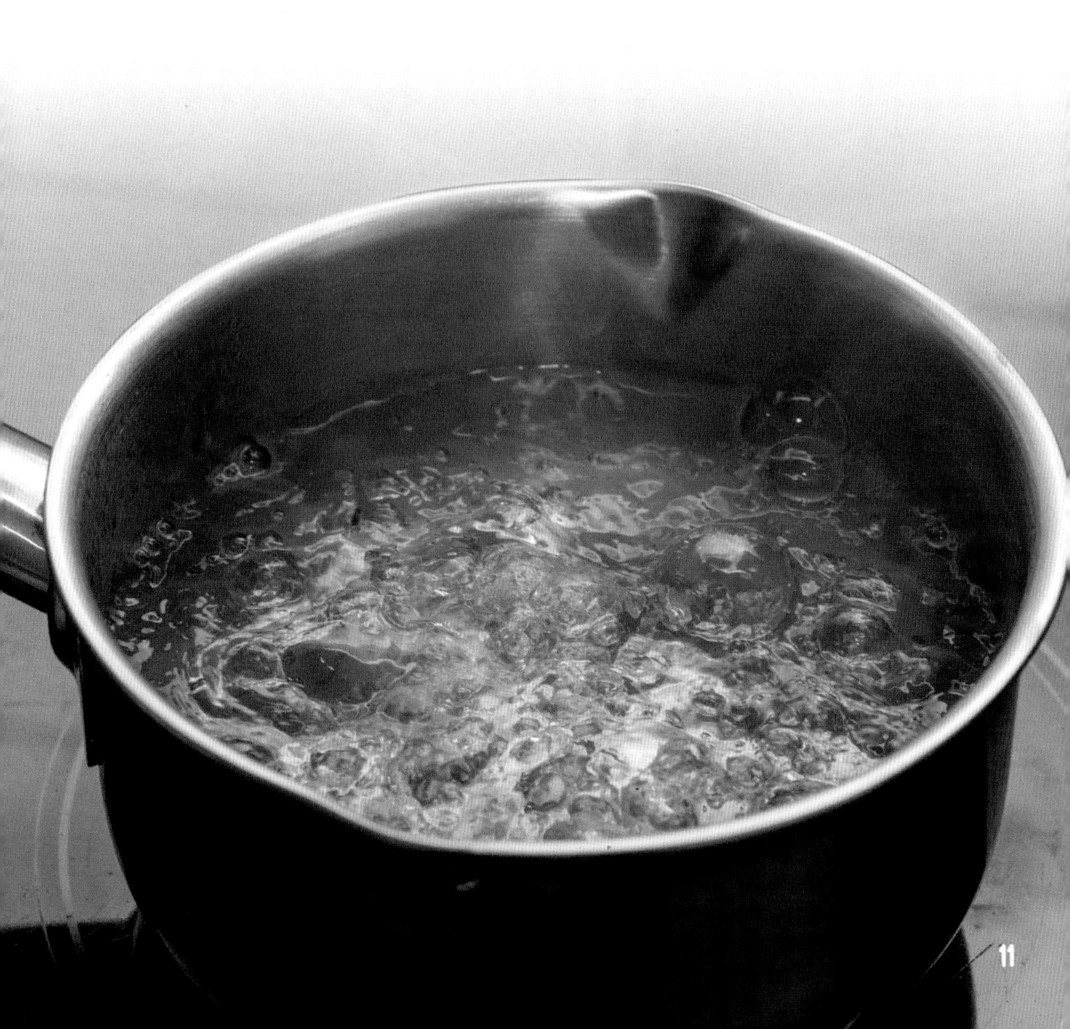

Meg set the egg
in the pot.

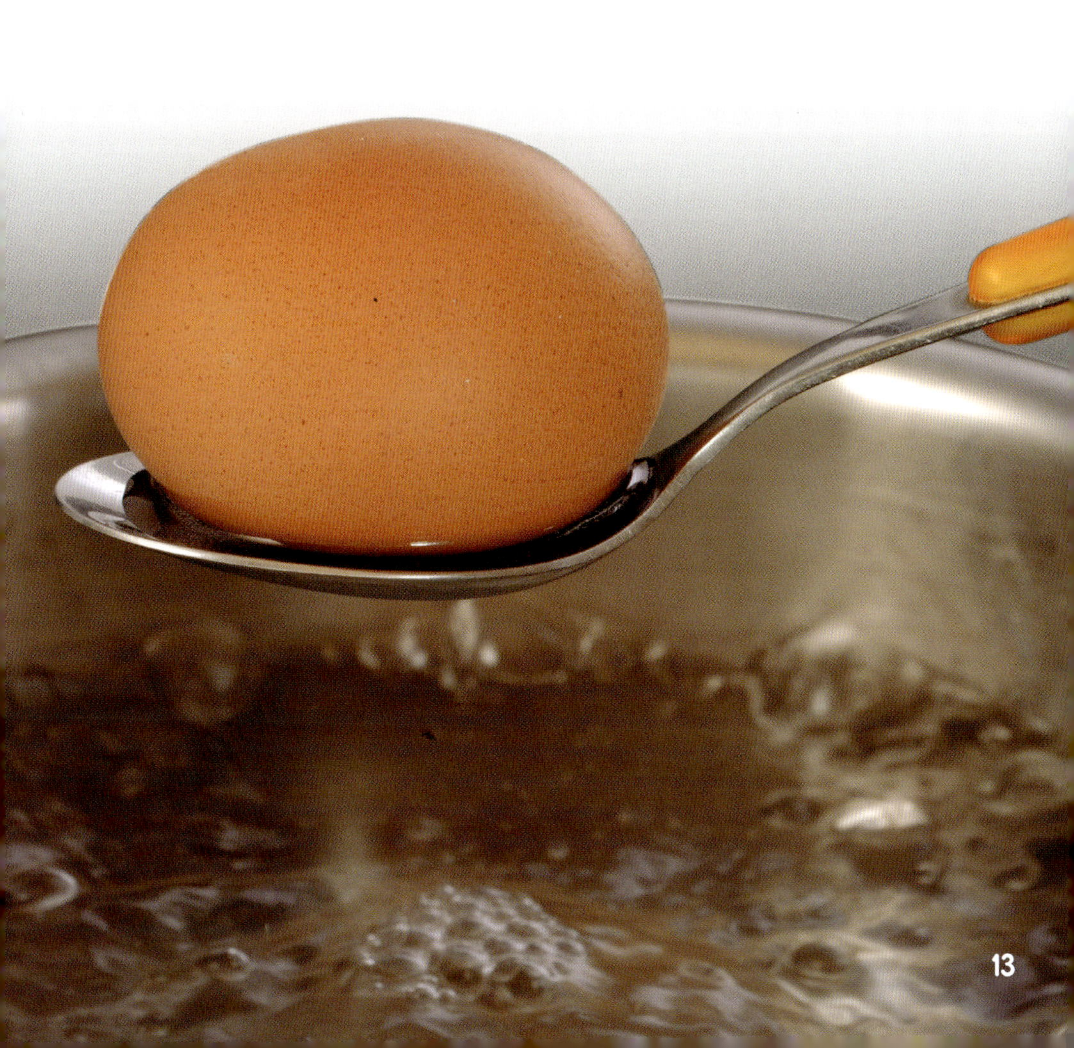

Meg had the egg.

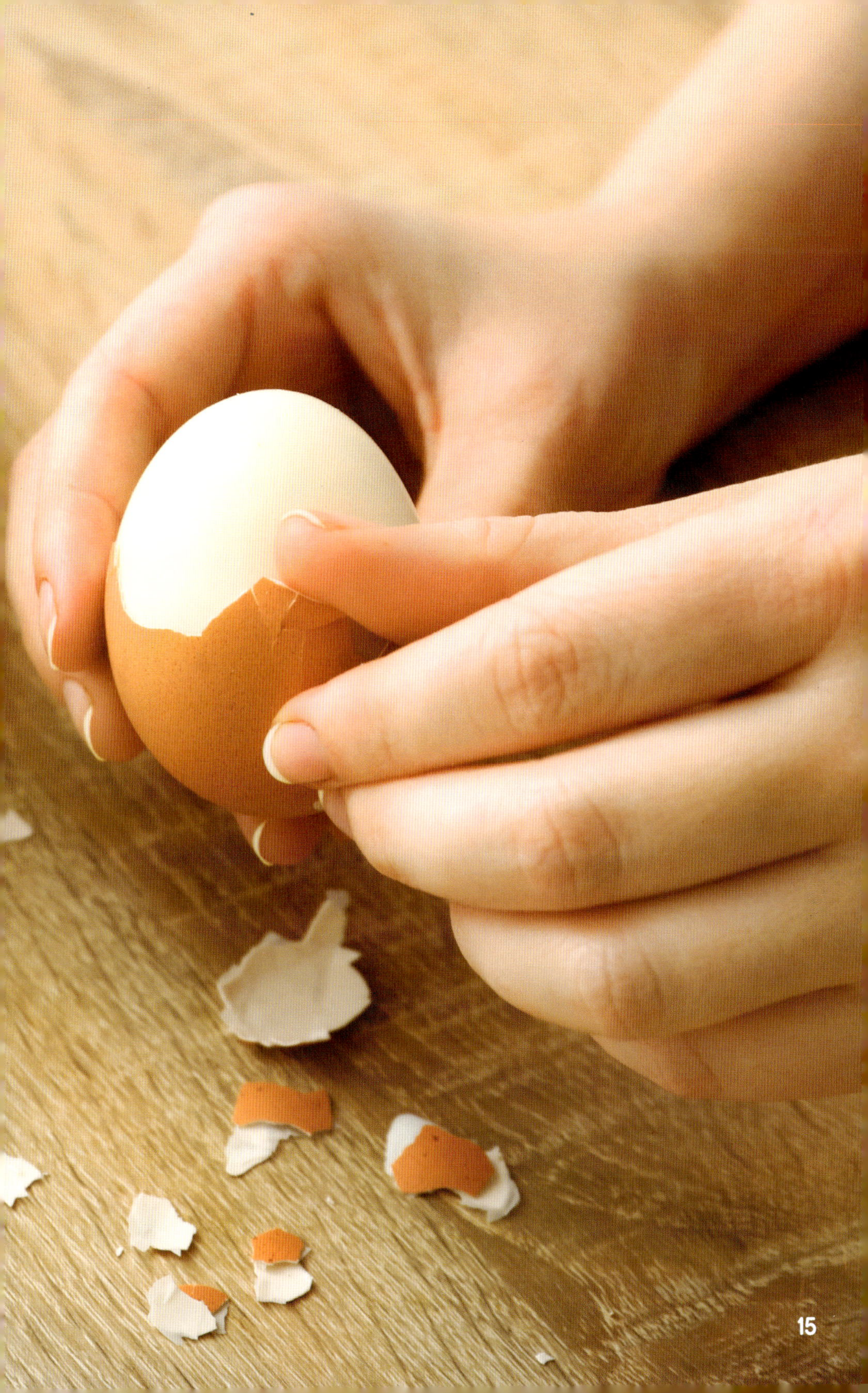

egg(s)	let	set
get	Meg	ten
hen		

an	had	in
cup	hot	pot
got		

a	for	the